StoneSoup

Writing and art by kids, for kids

Editor's Note

Leaves turning red, orange, and yellow as they dry out and fall off the branches. Days getting shorter, the air turning cold. Like spring, fall is a season of transition. When we are in winter and summer, we are *in* them. But we are never truly in the transitional seasons; the weather is constantly shifting, the temperature inching up or down.

In these transitional seasons, I always find myself thinking about change and about time. Now we have devices everywhere that tell us the time—our computers, our phones, our smart watches, our microwaves, our ovens, and our cars. But before all those devices, and before clocks, there was the natural world—the seasons to tell us what time of year it is, and the sun and the moon to tell us what time of day or night.

The art and writing in this issue encompass a range of topics and styles, but all of the pieces circle, in some way, these essential questions: How does time change us? How do we change in time? And how do we make sense of these changes over time?

Enjoy the witching season!

On the cover:
Baleful Strix
(Colored pencil, pastel, acrylic, and watercolor)
Zoe Campbell, 11
San Francisco, CA

Editor in Chief
Emma Wood

Director
William Rubel

Managing Editor
Jane Levi

Design
Joe Ewart

Blog Editor
Caleb Berg

Engagement Editor
Malakai Wade

Customer Service
Tayleigh Greene

Special Projects
Sarah Ainsworth

Refugee Project & Book Club
Laura Moran

Interns
Anya Geist, Ryan Hudgins, Claire Jiang, Sage Millen, Sim Ling Thee

Stone Soup (ISSN 0094 579X) is published eleven times per year—monthly, with a combined July/August summer issue. Copyright © 2021 by the Children's Art Foundation–Stone Soup Inc., a 501(c)(3) nonprofit organization located in Santa Cruz, California. All rights reserved.

Thirty-five percent of our subscription price is tax-deductible. Make a donation at Stonesoup.com/donate, and support us by choosing Children's Art Foundation as your Amazon Smile charity.

To request the braille edition of *Stone Soup* from the National Library of Congress, call +1 800-424-8567. To request access to the audio edition via the National Federation of the Blind's NFB-NEWSLINE®, call +1 866-504-7300, or visit Nfbnewsline.org.

StoneSoup
Contents

Girl with a Camera (iPhone SE)
Eliana Pacillo, 12
Walpole, MA

Autobiographical Vignettes

The author reflects on the rain, on God and the nature of life, on becoming an older sister and the pandemic

By Anushka Trivedi, 10
Silver Spring, MD

EMPEROR MONSOON

The rain looks like crystallized icicles falling in gray sheets from the sky. The earth moves with its impact. Every other sound is subdued, as if bowing down respectfully to Emperor Monsoon.

I watch from the window of my grandparents' home in the city of Ahmedabad, India. The plants dance as the cascade of water washes off layers of dust from their delicate leaves. The rains have breathed life into them. Green looks greener, grey looks greyer, red looks redder, white looks whiter. Water has colored the world.

About a dozen langur monkeys are escaping into the branches before they are completely drenched, leaping from roof to roof, balcony to balcony, with confidence and ease. They never miss a step or make a mistake. Tiny baby monkeys clutch their mothers' bellies. They do not have a care in the world. They are safe as they glide above the world with their family.

The stray dogs scurry away as well. They welcome the cool water on their overheated backs but prefer the shaded garage or the space under the cars. They want to hear the rain and feel the earth cool off before they venture out again.

I cannot resist feeling the rain on my skin. I skip to the patio and watch the drenched swing swinging gently by itself in the rain. Even the wood and metal on the swing seem grateful for the cool water on their burning bodies. I reach out and feel the drops on my palms. Slowly, I move forward beyond the shade of the patio and feel the rain thundering on my body. I feel like I am standing under a waterfall. I am completely wet in seconds. There is no stopping me now. I jump in the small puddles that rain has created on the patio, kick water into the air, and raise my face to the sky in utter delight. I skip, hop, and sing in the rain.

DUTY

"Arjuna, everyone depending on his or her station in life has a certain dharma to perform. You are a warrior. Your Dharma is to fight for a righteous cause."
— *The Bhagavad Gita*

These words are spoken by Krishna in the Bhagavad Gita. The Bhagavad Gita (meaning "the song of God" in Sanskrit) is a Hindu scripture that is a part of the *Mahabharata*, an ancient Hindu epic. It is a conversation between Prince Arjuna, a Pandava prince, and Krishna, who is an avatar, or incarnation, of Lord Vishnu, one of three supreme and divine deities in Hinduism.

My parents are atheists. They are raising my sister and me as atheists. This means that even though we celebrate many Hindu traditions and festivals, my parents do not believe in the existence of God. I have asked many times, ever since I was even younger than I am now, why they don't believe in God. They reply matter-of-factly that there is no evidence or argument to suggest that any gods exist. They tell me that it is okay to believe in God, but that does not mean that there is a god.

"Your beliefs don't make things exist, or make them real," they respond critically.

What they say is discouraging for me. For many years, I had given up on these questions about God and just behaved like them. My grandparents, however, do believe in God. My trips to India over the years have given me a different perspective about this question. My grandparents pray in front of their temples in their homes every morning and evening. They light a lamp and incense stick and offer flowers and food to the deities. They sing Sanskrit hymns and meditate. Seeing their rituals and practices makes me wonder why my parents are atheists when they could be part of such beautiful and ancient customs and mythologies.

I have asked my grandparents the same question: "Why do you believe in God?" My *dadi* (my father's mother) told me that God is everywhere and God is within you. God is like a friend who is there to help you when you need it. That makes me wonder whether prayers have the power to help me through my problems.

I have always been curious about these questions, and they have never really let me go. Since I had a lot of time and many things to worry about during the pandemic, I began to explore the many books we have on the topmost shelves of our house and to ask some new questions. Over the years, my grandparents have gifted me many books on Hindu mythology and philosophy. This spring and summer, I had the chance to dig into them.

I think I have some new arguments for my parents after many hours of reading and thinking. Here they go:

(1) There are many things that we don't see, like our thoughts and feelings, but that does not mean they don't exist.

(2) I don't think that every question should be answered with science. There are other types of knowledge

in this world, like what you get by experiencing something.

(3) It does not matter what you call God, or whether it has some form, or whether it exists. I think these are the wrong questions. I think a better question would be "What is God? What does it mean to you?" For me, hope, love, and courage are God.

Reading these epics and mythological stories has opened my mind to new ways of seeing the world. They have changed my perspective. They have given me hope, courage, and perseverance that I never knew before. It makes me feel happier than without this hope, courage, and perseverance. For that reason, I want to believe in the existence of God.

It is said in the Hindu scriptures that only if you open your mind to knowledge will you receive the knowledge. I understand how this can be true. When I was like my parents—not believing God—I didn't know the things I know today. I know that belief can open your mind to new ways of seeing the world. I know that I have a duty to perform in my life. Right now, my duty is to be content with whatever I have.

PINING FOR A LITTLE SISTER

Since I was three years old until I was about four and a half, so the legend goes, I demanded, pleaded, and prayed for a little sister. Every single morning, I asked my mom the same question: "Do you have a baby in your tummy today?" The answer was an exasperated "No" every single day.

Again, I would pray before drifting off to sleep to "please give me a little sister soon." I am known for not giving up.

I wanted a sister so badly that I announced to anyone who would care to listen in pre-K that "My mommy has a baby in her tummy." It seemed that everyone around me had a little brother or sister, or if they were very lucky, both! I was missing out on something major in life. My pre-K teachers told my parents how good I was with babies even when I was a toddler myself. I loved to watch them, make them laugh, and do whatever I could to help them. Naturally, I did not want to be left out of this life-changing experience.

People would congratulate my parents, and they would have to tell them that this was not true. I wanted it to be true, so it did not really matter whether it was true or not. It was true to me. My parents seemed perplexed and amused at how single-minded I was in this demand. They thought it was just a whim and I would get over it in week, a few weeks, or months. Not me! For the next two-and-a-half years, I persisted. The thought of failure never even occurred to me.

I remember that magical winter day when my parents announced, "You are going to be a big sister!" I was overjoyed.

The funny thing is that when I learned that I was going to have a sister, I kept it a secret and told no one until she was born.

THE BIRTH OF SAMIRA

It was a lovely fall day. The leaves were beginning to turn. Some leaves fell gently to the ground in the light September breeze. I was going to be a sister any day now. I had waited so long, watching my mother's belly grow, imagining what my sister would be like. My parents told me how big she must be each month. She had grown from the size of a sesame seed to a pomegranate seed, to a pea, to a peanut, to an orange, to the size of my palm, to a baby with tiny arms and legs, to a baby with fingernails, to a soccer ball, to a watermelon, to a baby with a tail, to a baby with no tail and a head full of hair! It was such a mystery. Ever since I saw her on the screen as the doctor checked my mother, I could not wait any longer. It looked like she was giving me a "thumbs up" on the screen that day. *She knows I am watching her*, I thought. *She knows I am her big sister*, I imagined. *I can't wait to see you, Samira.*

The September breeze blew on my face as I looked outside the bus window on my way back from school that day. It was the first couple of weeks of kindergarten, and it was not what I had expected. One of the things that shocked me most about school was how much we had to sit and how little we talked or played. I was full of questions about everything, but I felt I never got the chance to ask any of them. Getting on the bus to get back home was the best part of my day. I had memorized the route from school to the bus stop. I found a window seat and knew it was my stop when I saw either my grandpa, dad, or mom waiting for me at a distance. If it was my mom, it was my routine to jump out of the bus and give her belly a big hug and kiss, and greet Samira.

The bus was noisy, as it was every day. It was one of the several things that bothered me about school. How loud the day could be! I longed to get back to my room and immerse myself in my toys for the next few hours until I had forgotten all about school.

When is Samira going to be born? I have waited and waited and waited.

I ignored the loud children and looked through the bus window. I watched the birds perched on the trees and flying through the sky and let the noises dissolve in the background.

Little did I know that today was the day I would become a sister. Samira was born a sister; I became one that day.

When my stop arrived, the kids stormed out of the bus. I walked out of the bus quietly when I got the chance and jumped into my grandpa's arms. His face looked different that day. It looked bright and happy, maybe relieved. As we walked home, he told me that he had a surprise to share with me. My sister was born, and she and my mama and *baba* were in the hospital waiting for me. I could not believe it!

"When do I get to go see her?" I exclaimed. I think I flew home from the bus stop in joy that day.

At home, my grandma gave me a snack, and I waited for my dad to pick my grandparents and me up to go to the hospital. It seemed like a long wait, but it was actually only an hour or so. I remember swinging my legs from side to side with excitement when we finally got in the car to go to the hospital. Is there a word for the excitement you feel when you wait for a joyous occasion? I have felt this excitement often—waiting for the airplane to land at the Ahmedabad airport so I can see my grandparents' faces; waiting for the airplane to land at the Dulles airport to see my grandparents' faces when they come to visit us; looking out of the train window to see my cousins' faces in Pune; waiting in daycare for my parents to return from the university. This feeling of waiting for that one moment of joy. I have had a lot of training in the art of waiting. Waiting patiently is a good way to be for a child.

At last! I saw my mother sitting up on the hospital bed. She looked like she had been waiting for me too. She looked the same as she had in the morning when she waved me goodbye. She looked contented. I gave her a big hug and a kiss and just rested for a few moments.

But I quickly remembered to turn my gaze to her right. There she was. *How tiny she is!* That was my first thought. She was wrapped tight like a mummy, complete with a little pink-and-blue-striped hat. Her eyes were tight shut. She had, and still does have, the longest, thickest, curviest eyelashes of all. Her little mouth was like a flower bud, so beautifully shaped. Her cheeks were out of this world—round and smooth. She looked just like me. I was amazed at how much she resembled me. Everyone agreed.

I did not say a word and continued to observe her until my dad lifted her and placed her in my lap as I sat down. I cannot forget the feeling of holding her for the first time. She seemed heavy for such a tiny thing. I quickly got used to it. I touched her cheeks, and they were as smooth as the porcelain teacups Mama takes out for special guests. I whispered, "Samira." She opened her eyes! Her eyes were enormous on her little face that was smaller than a small bowl. They were the prettiest eyes I had seen. She looked straight into my eyes, and we exchanged unspoken words. I heard her say, "I am here. We are going to have a lot of fun. I am going to be so naughty. Get ready!" She opened her little mouth to yawn, and her toothless mouth made me giggle. "I am ready, Samira. I have a friend for life. Thank you for coming. I love you so much."

And so began the years of companionship. I have watched Samira grow and change and develop over the years—from her first smile to her very first day of kindergarten. She is the only friend I need.

A TEARFUL DAY

Some thoughts are difficult to think. They are even more difficult to put on paper. In September 2019, I experienced the most horrifying moment of life. My little sister, Samira, had celebrated her fourth birthday a few days ago. She was due for her yearly visit to the doctor and her last round of shots. My parents usually took us both to the doctor at the same time for our checkups. So I tagged along.

I watched Samira play with the toys in the waiting room in our doctor's office. She wanted me to play with her; she does not like to play on her own when I am around. I complied, as I always do, even though I would have liked to be quiet and think. Just then, the nurse called both our names. Samira looked nervous. She has always been suspicious of this place and everyone in it. Of course, she makes sure everyone knows how she feels. I took Samira's hand and walked with her, hoping that she did not create too much of a scene that day.

I was pleasantly surprised how cooperative Samira was during the initial part of the visit. Then came those dreadful shots. I got my flu shot first to show Samira that it would be alright. She was not at all convinced. Samira needed to get three shots to protect her against a number of diseases. She cried very loudly and was extremely distraught. It was over within minutes, or so we thought.

As my parents did some paperwork in the waiting room before we left, everything began to go wrong. Samira started sneezing violently. I have never seen her sneeze that way. It seemed as though a cup of snot came out of her nose, with over twenty-five sneezes in moments. She began to become drowsy. When my mom and dad tried to sit her down to wipe her nose, she could not even sit up. Her eyes began to close shut. Her face fell and turned pale. She seemed to fall asleep on my mother's shoulders.

My parents were stunned, and we rushed back inside the doctor's room. The next fifteen minutes were a blur of movement and people, tubes, oxygen tanks, and more shots. It seemed like I was still and everything around me was moving.

What is happening? What is going on?

My mom's eyes looked like glass stones. My dad was still, thinking and listening. I heard snippets like "... oxygen level going down," "... 60 percent," "... okay, it's rising ..." The doctor put me on her lap and rivers of tears flowed over. I don't remember what she said. Something kind and reassuring in a calm and soft voice. I closed my eyes and begged someone to save her, silently.

Suddenly, I heard the ambulance blaring. There was another rush of people and equipment. More shots and tubes. Samira was carried and put on a stretcher and lifted into the ambulance. My mom left with the ambulance. She did not have a chance to look at me. I heard someone say, "She's going to be okay." Did I hear it or did I imagine it? I do not know for sure. I heard my dad's soothing words, but I can't remember what they were. I calmed down in the car as my dad and I drove silently behind the ambulance.

When we reached the emergency room at the hospital, we ran to find Samira. Samira's eyes were open when I saw her. Her big, beautiful, bonny brown eyes. She had an oxygen mask around her face, and her skin was patchy and blue. She looked drained, but she was alive! She had survived. It was like opening my eyes after a nightmare to realize it was a dream. I felt I could breathe again.

I stayed with her for hours. I felt a surge of emotions. So much sadness for Samira and all the pain she was going through, relief that she was alive, anxiety about what would happen next and whether this would happen again, confusion about what had really happened, and a little bit of hope that something like this would never happen again.

The doctor told us that Samira needed to stay overnight. So my dad and I drove back home to gather some things like clothes, snacks, and toys. Back at the hospital, Mama and Samira looked much more like themselves by then. Samira was very hungry. She had not been given a thing to eat since breakfast. I was so happy to see her eat so gleefully.

After Mama and Samira finished eating, we all were taken to a room for the night. My dad and I made Samira comfortable and said goodnight. Samira didn't want us to leave. So we stayed till she fell asleep. After that, I hugged my mama tightly and left.

That night, my dad told me that I could sleep next to him. I lay down my head and drifted off to a dreamless sleep. The day had finally ended.

WHAT IS A FRIEND?

Unfortunately, I have met many careless people in my school life. Careless people are those who don't sacrifice anything for anyone, do only what they want, think only of themselves, and even in the hardest moments, ignore the pain of others. As a result, I have learned what friendship is.

You can recognize a friend only in time. Building friendship needs time. I have found that children my age are quick to "be friends" or become "best friends." However, these friendships fade away or break just as quickly. It's

"easy come, easy go." I prefer to take friendships slowly.

Affection is an important part of friendships. Affectionate friends are observant. They can see when you are sad or happy or in trouble, without you having to tell them. At the same time, affectionate friends use the right words at the right time. Saying the wrong words at the right time, or the right words at the wrong time—or the most damaging of all, the wrong words at the wrong time—can be hurtful. This past year I have experienced some of that. You can learn a person's true character by the words they use.

True friends stick up for each other because they trust each other. Friends ask questions rather than making assumptions. They listen rather than making judgements. They believe rather than doubt. Friends don't break each other's trust.

A final quality of friendship is its purpose. Some people just want to be your friend because they want something from you. True friends are not looking for "something" from you. They are looking for a supportive ear for their questions or troubles, a shoulder to rest on when they are tired, someone to talk things through, and someone to share a success or delightful moment. Such friends have been rare in my life.

THE WORLD HAS CHANGED

The Earth revolves on its axis. One day ends and the next begins. Time passes on as it always has. Winter turned into spring, spring turned into summer, and summer has turned into fall as it does every year. However, everything feels different. Everything is different. Will it ever be the same again?

The world around me is lost. The world is motionless. The Earth is round, but time is flat. For weeks, I could not play outside. I still have not gone swimming since spring 2019. I no longer go to school. I no longer see my teachers or friends, except through a screen. Everyone can be here, but not here. I am told to believe that we are connecting with each other through a computer. I feel farther apart from everyone and everything.

These are the most unusual of circumstances. The news came out of the blue. "Pandemic," "coronavirus," "COVID-19," "global health crisis," "deaths," "cases," and many more new words became part of my world. Suddenly, all schools, offices, shops, and restaurants were shut down. Everyone was asked to "stay home," leaving only for essentials or emergencies. Everyone was asked to wear face masks and gloves when they had to be outside among others. We are told there is an "invisible enemy" which we can defeat only by staying apart from each other.

While my family and I stayed safe inside our home, apart from the world around us, we depended on millions of others to keep this world moving on. I have felt lucky and guilty at the same time. I have probably learned more things through this experience than I have ever before.

I have learned how connected we are to the world around us. The coronavirus started in China but has spread quickly all over the world. Children all around the world are in the same situation as me. Millions of children's parents all across the world have lost their jobs. Many children have lost one or more of their family members to this virus.

I have learned how important leadership is, especially during such a life-threatening situation. We don't have good leaders in America. Our president through much of the pandemic made an already challenging problem even worse by lying and ignoring the problem.

I have learned that there is so much inequality in our country. Many people don't have health care, and now that they have lost their jobs, they can't go to the doctor if they fall ill.

I have learned that there is a lot of greed in our country. The health industry does not want to provide health care that people can afford. People hoarded food and toilet paper (toilet paper!) during this pandemic. The supermarket shelves were empty! I am scared to live in this kind of world—a world that is so fragile that a small push can topple everything down, a world that is so cruel and unjust.

I don't understand everything, and I am thankful that I don't. Unlike most grown-ups, I can always go back to the world of play and forget about my fears. Being away from school and everything else has given me the time to read, write, play, and think. Living through this global pandemic has allowed me to reflect on my experiences, my relationship to my sister, culture and faith, and my role in the world. I have learned that music, poetry, and companionship are the most important ingredients of my life.

Layers (iPhone 7)
Grace Williams, 12
Katonah, NY

Two Poems

By Julia Marcus, 13
Culver City, CA

Midnight

It must be
so lonely
to be a clock
in the middle
of the night
hanging
on the wall
steadily ticking
through the darkness
with no one
awake to ask:
What time is it?
even though
you will be able
to say
just the same.

Air

Fresh pine
and dust in the wind
with a touch
of flowers and sage
and the faraway glimmer
of Lake Alpine.

We've risen above
most of everything
and all of civilization
has abandoned us.

A hawk soars
in the thin air.
I think I am
that hawk.

I kick over a rock
and dirt enters my shoe.
The smell of trees
never fades.

Fountain (Canon PowerShot G15)
Oskar Cross, 10
Oakland, CA

Friends

Naomi and Oscar are best friends, and they do the same thing every day—or at least, they used to

By Raya Ilieva, 10
Belmont, CA

Naomi Keith's feet slapped the cracked pavement of the sidewalk. She scoured the streets of Cedar Key, their small Florida town, looking for any interesting people. Her best friend, Oscar Hernandez, walked next to her. Suddenly, she spotted a middle-aged woman wearing wrinkled khaki long pants, even in ninety-degree June weather, and a puffy black jacket. She had a baseball cap pulled low and her phone was shoved near her face. She looked rather cross. A perfect suspect.

Naomi nudged Oscar and pointed discreetly at the woman walking on the other side of the street. "That woman . . . is actually a certified genius. She attends an elite top college that almost nobody knows about, and she's one of five people there. She's working on designing an app like FaceTime but you only have to move your lips and the device you're using will read your lips and what you're saying will appear as text on the other person's screen." Naomi paused for a breath.

"She looks mad because the app isn't working right. Also, she has been working day and night on it and hasn't been able to get much sleep. She hasn't been able to change clothes, so that's

why her pants are wrinkled. Her face is close to the screen because . . . the translator isn't working and the other person is getting something like 'Pig sit docking?' instead of 'Is this working?' so she puts her mouth as close to the screen as possible."

Naomi grinned. That was her best one for the day yet, by far. She looked to Oscar for feedback, but to her surprise, he was looking longingly at the posse of popular boys who were monkeying around on the nearby skate park.

"Oscar! Did you even listen to my story? It was the best one yet," Naomi said, annoyed.

"What? Oh, yeah, it was good." But Naomi could tell that he hadn't really been listening.

"Um, hey, Naomi?" Oscar said suddenly, after a minute of awkward silence.

"Yeah?" Naomi said, thinking he meant to apologize.

"Um, would you mind if I join those guys over there?" He jerked his thumb over to the direction of the skate park, taking Naomi by surprise.

"But . . . you don't skate," was all Naomi could manage to get out.

Is it possible that he thinks that being friends with a girl when we're twelve is weird?

"I'm sure I can borrow one of the guys' boards. Please, Na? Just today. We'll walk again tomorrow."

"Sure..." Naomi replied uncertainly. But she wasn't so certain she wanted Oscar to go.

"Thanks, Na. You're the best," Oscar called.

"Yeah," Naomi mumbled once he was out of earshot. "But you still don't want to hang out with me."

Her feelings hurt, she trudged home, not even stopping for a mango smoothie to cool her down. After all, that was something she only did with Oscar. And clearly he didn't want to hang out with her anymore. He was her best (and only) friend. They had been playing together since preschool and would go on walks every day. As they walked, they would look at passersby and imagine stories about them. It was her favorite time of the day. She looked forward to being with Oscar. But now, apparently, he was ditching her for those crazy skateboarding boys.

She sighed in relief when she reached her house. "How was your walk?" her mother asked, wiping perspiration from her forehead. She had been cleaning out the attic for a garage sale, which was a taxing task.

"Mmm," Naomi mumbled, not wanting to talk about it. She shuffled up the stairs and into her room.

She closed her window, which was now just letting in the humid Florida summer air, and switched on her fan. It whirred to life and blew cold air at her sweaty face. She lined the fan up by her bed and flopped onto it to think, staring at the cracks and water stains in the ceiling as she did so.

Did I do something wrong? I don't think so. I was just telling a story about that woman, which was perfectly okay because just moments earlier he had been telling a story about that guy in his fancy Lexus zooming down the street way too fast. That was a funny one. Although come to think of it... it didn't have as much detail as Oscar's stories usually have. And he was kinda distracted as he told it. I thought he was just thinking about what to say next, but apparently not. And why would he want to hang out with the posse of popular boys? They're annoying and immature... and he doesn't even skate!

Naomi sighed and rubbed her temples. It was all so confusing! Suddenly, a new thought occurred to her: is it possible that he thinks that being friends with a girl when we're twelve is weird? She mulled this one over for quite some time, finally deciding that it was the most reasonable answer—but also the one that she liked the least. Why would it be weird? Everybody in their small Florida town knew that Oscar and Naomi were best friends. It was just a fact, like everyone knew little Mrs. White was widowed. It was just... a thing. Nobody acted weird if they saw Naomi and Oscar together.

She puzzled a little more until dinner, where she was unusually quiet. She focused on picking at her food, cold soba noodles with cabbage and pork, and keeping a bite in her mouth at all times.

That night, sleep did not come easily. Naomi tossed and turned, the events of the afternoon replaying themselves over and over in her mind. Eventually, at 11:30, she managed to fall into a light and fitful slumber.

The next morning, Naomi was in a foul mood. She had woken up early, at 6:00, and all in all got less than seven hours of sleep. Which, for a growing girl, was not much at all. At breakfast, she snapped at her younger twin brothers, talked back to her mom, and ignored her dad completely.

She moped around all day until 3:00, the hottest time of the day, and when she usually saw Oscar. Naomi trudged out of the house and walked a few houses down to Oscar's. Surely he'd have seen that those boys were nothing more than a rowdy, immature bunch not worth hanging out with. And anyway, he'd promised her that they'd walk today. Her hopes up, she rapped her fingers against the fading wood of the door to Oscar's house.

But while usually a smiling Oscar would greet her, now Mrs. Hernandez came to the door. This in and of itself was not a good sign.

"Hello, Naomi. And what brings you here today?" Mrs. Hernandez smiled.

"Um, actually, I was wondering where Oscar was? We usually go on walks this time of day, so . . ." Naomi trailed off uncertainly.

Mrs. Hernandez's face fell. "I'm sorry, Naomi. Oscar went to hang out with Aaron and Juan and their crew. He just left. He'll be back in an hour or two. Sorry." And with that, Mrs. Hernandez shut the door quietly, but firmly, in Naomi's face.

Naomi couldn't decide whether to be mad or sad. Oscar had promised her. He had said, "We'll walk again tomorrow."

She decided that even if Oscar was being a pill and not his usual self, that shouldn't stop her from walking and getting a smoothie. She started out on their usual route.

At first, walking without Oscar made her feel strange and a little guilty. But she soon shook the feelings off, deciding that she was more mad than sad.

Feeling adventurous, Naomi even took a detour from their usual route. Another thing about Oscar was that he was set in his ways. They had walked the exact same route every single day without fail, except when one of them was sick. Which wasn't very often. They knew the owner of the smoothie shack, Luis Marquez, and his son, Rodrigo, like old friends. They always ordered the same thing. So Naomi realized that it was very unlike Oscar to go hang with the posse. They had deemed those boys not worthy of their company and, well, they just weren't Naomi and Oscar's type.

Naomi realized that she had reached the smoothie shack. Rodrigo was lazing around by the counter— there were no other customers—and his dad was nowhere in sight.

A surprised look flickered across Rodrigo's face, but quickly dissipated. Naomi tried her best to ignore it, but it was hard.

"No Oscar today?" Rodrigo asked, as casually as possible.

"No, he's . . . sick," Naomi replied. She couldn't bring herself to tell Rodrigo the real truth.

He nodded. "Uh-huh." But there was a note of skepticism in his voice. Naomi brushed it off. "Your usual?" Rodrigo asked, even though it wasn't really a question anymore.

Naomi surprised herself by saying, "Nah, I'll try a raspberry-lime shake."

This time Rodrigo didn't even try to hide his surprise. "You sure?" he asked.

"Yeah," Naomi answered, sounding more confident than she really was.

"All right." Rodrigo turned around and whipped it up. When he handed it to her, Naomi regarded it with interest. It was pinkish red in color, with a bubbly lime-green top, and a thick straw stuck in the middle. Naomi picked it up from the counter, thanked Rodrigo, and walked coolly out the door, even though inside she was nearly shaking. Had she really just ordered a different thing than what she had ordered for three years straight? Yes, she told herself. She had.

She sipped at the raspberry-lime shake, delighted by the cool, slightly tangy but also sweet flavor. Naomi decided that she would order this from now on. It didn't matter what Oscar thought or did; she was her own person.

Naomi took the long route back home, wanting to savor her drink as much as she could. When she got home, her mom gave her a friendly nod and didn't ask how her walk was. Naomi nodded courteously back.

Her mom noticed the change in beverage. "Trying something new?" she asked.

"Yeah," Naomi replied. "It's really good. Do you want to try?"

Her mom nodded and took a sip, then smiled.

"Good, right?" Naomi asked.

"Yes, very. I'm glad to see you branching out."

Naomi just shrugged and smiled.

She spent the rest of the day reading in her room. She was a lot more civil at dinner and talked and laughed with her family. Her dad worked at the local hospital as a pediatrician. He usually had funny stories, and today was no exception.

"You know," he started, and Naomi and her two little brothers, Noah and Nate, perked up their ears and leaned forward. "You know how little kids are sometimes scared of the weirdest of things?" he continued. Naomi nodded and shot a meaningful glance at her two brothers. Noah was scared of butterflies and Nate was *terrified* of straws. Mr. Keith laughed and kept talking.

"Well, today, I had a five-year-old in the waiting room. Just as I was calling her and her mother into the office, in comes a lady with a big white lab, barking up a storm. He has on a vest—he's an emotional support dog. So this huge white lab starts barking at the five-year-old. Turns out she's terrified—and I mean TERRIFIED— of dogs. She climbs, literally climbs, up her mother's leg and into her arms. The mom has explained to me beforehand that her daughter is also terrified of shots. But when that dog comes in, the five-year-old asks, 'Can I get my shots now?' The mom is super surprised, but I say, 'Sure.' So I lead her to the room and we get her shots done. Turns out that dog traumatized her into getting her shots." Naomi's dad finished his story, and crossed his arms across his chest, a big grin on his face.

Naomi burst into laughter. Noah and Nate didn't really get the story, but when they saw their older sister laughing, they quickly started laughing too. It was a fun night, and Naomi slept better than she had yesterday. Still, the thought of Oscar ditching her for those boys hung in the air around her no matter how many times she tried to brush it away.

The next day passed the same way. Naomi was sort of hoping that Oscar would be back to his usual self, but she got the same response as last time from Mrs. Hernandez.

It was the same every time. Each time, Naomi felt a little sadder and a little worse, but she tried to brush it off.

She settled into a new routine. In the morning, she would open her window until it started to get humid and read. Then she would help make lunch, play with her brothers a bit, and go for a walk. She used her new route and now every time tried a new smoothie—although raspberry-lime was still her favorite.

She missed Oscar, but in a way it felt better not to have his routines weighing on her when she wanted to try something new. She saw him a few times monkeying around at the skate park but didn't make eye contact when he tried to.

At the end of the week, though, there was an unexpected knock at the door. Nobody ever knocked at the Keith household, not even Oscar. Naomi was the one who knocked on Oscar's door, always. Which was why she was surprised when there was a sharp rapping on the wood. Naomi sprang up from the kitchen table where she had been rereading one of her favorite series, *The Land of Stories*.

When she opened it, she was even more surprised to see Oscar standing there. Seeing him there made her feel mad all of a sudden, and she made a move to shut the door, but Oscar stopped it with his foot. "We need to talk, Naomi. Let's go for a walk." Naomi shrugged but reluctantly complied.

Silently, they made their way down the streets of their small town. After a minute, Oscar began to talk. "Look, Naomi, I really like hanging out with the guys. I mean, you're still my friend—"

"Friend? *Friend?* You said that first day that you would walk the next day and you haven't walked with me all week! You're never home, and you act like you hardly even know me!" Naomi cut him off, her voice rising to a shriek. Oscar hung his head, but Naomi refused to succumb to the gesture.

Instead, she led him on her new route.

"What? Since when do we go this way?" he asked, confused and distraught.

"Since you stopped hanging out with me," Naomi answered testily.

When they ended up at the smoothie shack, after another few minutes of awkward silence, Naomi ordered raspberry-lime.

"But I thought you ordered mango. Always," Oscar said meekly.

"Not anymore. And anyway, I only ordered mango because of you! I only went on that same route day after day because of *you! I AM MY OWN PERSON!*" Naomi faced him, her hands on her hips. "You . . . you . . . you . . . UGH!" And she stalked away, leaving Oscar staring at her retreating back and Rodrigo looking utterly confused.

Naomi started out walking and then broke into a run, ignoring the heat and humidity hanging over Florida like a cloud. How dare Oscar call her a friend when he himself had been ignoring her completely for the past five days! It made her broil.

She reached her small house and slammed the door behind her, collapsing at the kitchen table. Her mom, who had just finished cleaning out the attic, came down the stairs to find her daughter slumped on a chair with her forehead on the table, sobbing uncontrollably.

She sat down next to Naomi and waited until her sobs had subsided and she was only hiccupping occasionally to ask, "What's the matter, my girl?"

"H-h-he-he said I was a friend." And Naomi began to sob once more.

"Who said you were a friend? Why is that bad?" Her mother prodded, trying to get the full story.

"O-Oscar. He asked me one day if he could hang out with the popular boys at the skate park, saying we would walk tomorrow, but he kept hanging out with them and then . . ." The story poured out of Naomi, and her mother listened. At the end, her mother reached in for a hug and Naomi sank into her arms.

They continued to talk and eventually came to the conclusion that Naomi should apologize and voice her feelings reasonably. Even though what Naomi really wanted to do was yell at Oscar and never stop, she agreed that talking it out was probably the best idea.

For now, though, Naomi went up to read and think things over. She helped her mother make dinner to clear her head. It was surprisingly fun. Naomi vowed to do it more. She went to bed easily and slept soundly that night.

At 3:00 sharp, Naomi arrived at Oscar's house. She squared her shoulders and knocked. This time, when she asked Mrs. Hernandez for Oscar, he appeared instantly, as if he had been waiting for her. *Maybe he had*, thought Naomi.

She led Oscar on their new route and started talking. "Oscar . . . you've hurt my feelings. I didn't like it when you started hanging out with Aaron and Juan and the boys and not keeping your promises. That first day you said, 'We'll walk again tomorrow.' Did we? No. And not the next day or the next."

Naomi kept talking. She didn't stop until she was out of breath and Oscar finally had time to get a word in. "Naomi . . . I'm sorry. I just . . . maybe we shouldn't have such a set schedule? I love being your friend, Naomi, and you'll always be my best friend. But can you try to accept that Juan and Aaron are *my* friends now too?"

Naomi sighed. "Yes . . . it's just, they're immature and annoying and monkeying around. I thought we agreed they weren't worth our time."

"Naomi, they're really nice once you get to know them. It's fun hanging out with . . . different people sometimes."

When she saw him talking and laughing with them as they showed him a skateboard trick, she thought, Maybe those boys aren't so bad after all.

They kept up the talk like this until they had walked their usual loop twice. On the second time, they stopped at the smoothie shack. And Oscar tried raspberry-lime, at Naomi's prompting. "Hmm," he said, but a smile played at his lips and Naomi knew he liked it.

Once they reached Oscar's house, he said, "Naomi, I know I haven't been the best friend to you, and I'm sorry. I really am." He turned to go in, but Naomi stopped him.

"Wait—don't go. Maybe we can work out a compromise?" Naomi said.

"What kind of compromise?" Oscar asked.

"Like, maybe on Monday and Thursday and Saturday we can walk and on Tuesday and Friday and Sunday you can hang with the boys— Wednesday we can decide what to do? Something like that?"

"Sounds good," Oscar replied. He popped her a thumbs up and Naomi knew that everything was all right.

When Naomi walked through the door with a grin on her face and a confident air about her, her mother knew that their strategy had gone all right and things were good. She smiled.

The next day, Naomi allowed Oscar to hang out with the boys. When she saw him talking and laughing with them as they showed him a skateboard trick, she thought, *Maybe those boys aren't so bad after all.* And she knew that Oscar was having fun with them. She waved, a warm feeling settling in her stomach. It was all good.

A Tangled World (iPhone 8)
Elodie Weinzierl, 11
Waban, MA

Oak

By Graham TerBeek, 10
Towson, MD

Hello.
My name is Oak.
And if you didn't already guess, I am a tree.
I've heard rumors of trees that grow delicious fruit,
Of trees that bloom exotic flowers,
Or even trees that are so tall that it seems they can see the whole world.
It must be nice having a purpose.
I don't have anything special about me.
Just your typical, everyday tree.

I live in the backyard of a small house.
People rarely go in and out.
I keep to myself.
I don't mind, really.
I'm used to being alone.
Years ago, I wasn't alone.
I had a beautiful friend named Marigold living right next to me.
I don't like to think about her.
When the snow came, she passed.
Now I don't have friends.

Seasons passed,
The grass grew,
And eventually,
The people moved away.
I didn't really mind.
It wasn't that different.
It's just life.

I watched the sun.
Up and down and up and down.
Time passed.
I stood.
Waiting.
For what? I don't know.
But soon, I found out.
A new family moved in.
They trimmed my branches,
They cut the grass,
And best of all,
They brought new life.

A flower sprouted next to me.
Her name was Rose.
We talk.
She reminds me of Marigold.
And sometimes the other trees join in too.
There's this tree I like.
Birch is his name.
He makes Rose laugh.
I laugh too.
And realize how long it's been since I laughed.

But time passes.
Leaves fall.
Snow coats the ground,
Coating Rose too.
I shouldn't ever have made her my friend.
I care too much.
And,
Well,
I think you understand.

The snow has coated my branches.
This is the coldest winter I've ever been through.

Birch tries to make me laugh.
I try to laugh,
But I can't.

But the world moves on,
Winter passes,
Snow melts.
Spring takes over,
Bringing new life.
I take a deep breath.
"Rose?" I say, "You're back?"
"I never left," she says.

Seasons pass.
I notice all the birds chirping,
The bees buzzing,
I sleep.

I wake up to a rustling.
I see small children climbing me.
I wish I could shake them off.
But then I realize,
That I could have a purpose.
Soon I go back to sleep.
But I am woken up by a loud chirping.
I look in my highest branch
And see a mother bird feeding her young.
I look down and see worms burrowing through my roots,
And even a young man using my shade to read.

You see, I've heard rumors of trees that grow delicious fruit,
Of trees that bloom exotic flowers,
Or even trees that are so tall that it seems they can see the whole world.
And I have a purpose too.
People climb me,
They use my shade,
I am a home,
And best of all,
I am a friend.

Now, I stand up a little bit straighter,
A little bit taller,
I never knew how much there was to see.
Of course, I never really looked.

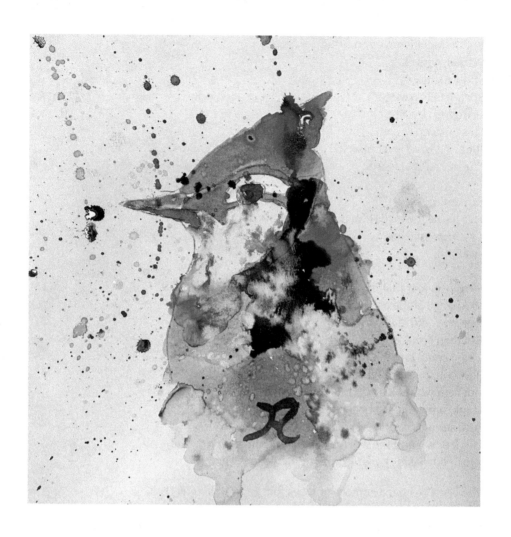

Blue Jay (Watercolor)
Aspen Clayton, 11
Lisle, IL

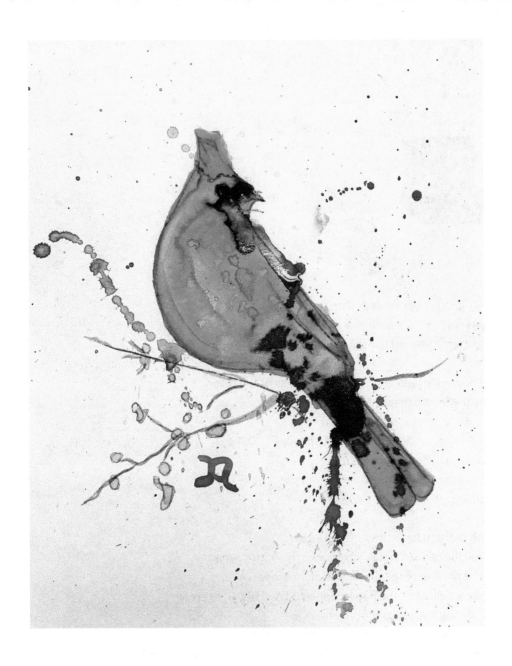

Cardinal (Watercolor)

Two Poems

By Sofie Dardzinski, 9
Potomac, MD

Moonlight

My gentle fingers landed on the heavy strings
as I saw the round circles
spiraling around the shining strings

The golden light entered the darkness of the room
as my thumb pricked the chilling string

My hands switched rapidly to the
next strings as I started to play a
sweet song, high notes and low notes
echoing throughout the room

All the light faded away from sight
and the sad low notes mixed with the happy ones
The rhythm of the music wrapped around me
like a quilt as all the notes connected and began to create
the song that glowed inside me
The music flowed in bouncy vibrating waves
until I didn't think about playing music at all on my elegant guitar
I just let the glowing music play out
of my mind and of my heart.

Time

Nobody knows what time is.
Time stretches everywhere
at different speeds, in peculiar shapes.

In space, time expands with the universe.
The speed of light is time—
we just can't see it.

Soaring, vibrating, flashing,
time can escape on feathered wings.
Time has a mind of its own; it has a reason
for what it chooses to do.

On Earth, time slinks away
when we don't pay attention.
Time is valuable, a privilege to have.

People say they can tell time
looking at clocks.
But we don't really know if that's time.
What is time to infinity?

The movement of time ripples through space,
connecting with other planets,
speeding up and slowing down,
expanding and contracting.

Time came from the beginning of life
and it will move on, sweeping
humans, animals, living beings with it.

In the end, the only thing we
really need to know about time
is what we do with it.

Aspiration (Pastel and watercolor)
Audrey Li, 12
Scarsdale, NY

Treacherous Climb

Kate and her pet mouse set out to scale colossal, rocky Mt. Treacherous

By Sarah Süel, 10
San Diego, CA

"Squeak!"

I was feeding my pet mouse, Hammy, some savory cheese I'd ripped off my sandwich. My eyes, as blue as the sea that peeked over the top of the trees and poked around the mountain that loomed above us, gazed affectionately at him. His cheeks were ballooned up, his eyes were bright and full of life, his fluffy grey fur was glowing in the morning sun, and his tiny but sharp claws held the cheese tight. I was sitting with my legs crossed on a bench as rough as sandpaper, but it never had given me a splinter. I wore a light dress and simple shoes. My cheeks were as pink as a rose, and my hair went from brown to a gold like the sun when it has just risen. I wore earrings the color of the lovely lavender that grows in a clearing in the forest; they are made out of a pearl and shaped into a heart. I had my hair in a braid to keep it neat while I worked.

After we were done with our breakfast, I put Hammy in my pocket and went out to milk the cow.

I came back a few minutes later holding two buckets full of milk that looked like the milk that comes out of a dandelion stem when you pull it out of the ground to make a wish. I gave the buckets to my mother to strain and make into cheese.

I went outside and grabbed a dandelion. I blew a warm stream of air at it and watched the fluffy seeds float into the sky till they disappeared. I gazed across the freshwater lake that was right outside our village. As I gazed there, I remembered that I wished for an adventure and, if I looked, I would find one. And if I did, I would be ready.

At dusk I sat on the bench and gazed outside at the mountain above us. Then an idea popped into my head like popcorn does when it's roasted over a fire. I would climb that mountain! It didn't have an official name, but most people called it Mt. Treacherous. Maybe because not everyone who climbed up climbed down, or was seriously injured, or fell off the mountain. But those thoughts didn't stop me!

That night I grabbed Hammy and a backpack with water, food, blankets as soft as a sheep, a flashlight, a strong rope, and mouse food.

As I was walking to the door, my

dad asked, "Where are you going?"

I replied as calmly as I could, "On an adventure."

"Well, good luck," he responded.

I ran through the forest and stopped at the mountain. It was even bigger standing right next to it. As I started up, a wrecking ball of wind hit me and knocked my backpack off. I managed to grab it, but when I jerked it out of the sky, the rope, some of Hammy's food, and one of the wool blankets fell out and got blown to who knows where. At first, I almost gave up, but then I encouraged myself and kept going. Making it to a ledge, I curled up like a pill bug with Hammy still in my pocket and fell asleep. When I woke up, I went on. I walked for a bit, then started climbing the steep wall.

Sweat dripped down my forehead and stung my eyes. I didn't once peek down at the ground, for I knew I would fall and hit my head on the rocks that stuck out from the cliff. Though without them, I would never have been able to climb up this steep slope. My arms and legs were tingling like they do when your foot is asleep, yet this time they were tingling from tiredness.

I could see the top of the cliff—I was so close!

I was so pumped by seeing the top that I didn't notice that the ledge I was reaching for was covered in yucky-colored moss, and it was like water to hold on to. My hand slipped, sending me wobbling, and I lost my footing on the ledge. I fell down fast! The wind was echoing in my ears, and I felt so helpless. I thudded in a thick bush that stopped me from getting anything more than a few scratches and some bruises the color of the sky at sunset.

When I tried to stand up, I got pulled back down to the ground and quickly saw that my foot was caught in a branch. I jerked my leg to get it unstuck. Though I was successful, I lost my balance. I could feel Hammy's toothpick-like claws grabbing my pocket and squeaking up a storm. I fell off the ledge and into a river.

"Wow, we sure are lucky!" I said to Hammy after grasping the side.

The water made me shiver from my spine, and even more when the cold wind hit me. I scanned the surrounding area and saw a path that was pretty narrow and steep with shrubs surrounding it. The climb was still hard, but it was easier than going back the way we came. As I glanced around absorbing the lovely scenery, I thought, *Maybe everything will work out.* And with that, I went on.

I trudged up the steep slope with Hammy in my pocket, still shivering from his dip in the river.

"That river felt like liquid ice!" I said, drying my hair.

Hammy squeaked in agreement.

As we climbed higher, we saw fewer trees and bushes. We mostly saw small, sun-beaten shrubs clinging onto the rocky edges.

It was getting late. A cool evening breeze dried off my soaking hair and ruffled Hammy's dense, grey fur. I scaled a rocky slope and sat down on a ledge, partly sheltered by some lush bushes. I took Hammy out of my pocket and stroked his soft fur. His fur might be the softest thing in the world—it's like a cloud, or cotton candy for your fingers. I stroked him till he was fully dry, then I sat him on my knee.

About a minute later, I was standing on the top of the mountain, proud as a sailor who had just discovered a new island.

Together we watched the ocean swallow the sun and the sun fight back with his rays of vivid colors. The ocean and mountain appeared to be on fire, glowing peach, papaya, and mango. Then the sun winked green to say goodbye and sank fully into the ocean. Hammy and I gazed into the dimming, vast blue stretch of the sea till we fell asleep. We slept peacefully under the glow of the Milky Way, sparkling in the cool, pitch-black night.

I was rudely awakened by the mountain growling, or by what I thought at first was the mountain growling. But I shook off the sleepiness and got to my wits—there was a rockslide!

I stood up and quickly threw everything into my backpack and slung it on my back. I gently, but quickly, put Hammy in my pocket and ran up to the ledge above where I had seen a small hole in the rocks and squeezed in. The squeeze made me feel like a lemon getting squeezed into lemonade. Lucky for me, the cave widened out into a huge chamber. Now there was just one small problem: the rockslide had blocked the tunnel entrance and we were trapped!

Just as I was about to panic, I heard a whine that didn't belong to Hammy. I moved behind a stalagmite that looked like a claw coming out of the ground. I beamed my flashlight around and spotted something that made my heart leap.

"There's a bear here!" I told Hammy, my eyes wide. "But it's just a cub! Maybe it got trapped here like us!"

I watched the bear sniff around and start to gallop away. Then an idea popped into my head.

"The bear cub will go toward its mother's scent, and its mother, to my understanding, is outside the cave!" I shouted out. "So, let's follow that cub!"

Staying out of sight, I walked behind the cub and saw that I had been right! The cub had found a small crack in the wall. He went through the hole, and Hammy and I followed. I ducked behind a tree to avoid being seen by the mother bear, whom the cub had found. I slipped by without, thankfully, being seen by the bears.

When I was far away from the bears, I looked up for the first time. I was so close to the top! But there was such a steep slope, I would never be able to get there. I sat on the dirt. I felt like a piece of paper that someone crumpled and put into the trash.

As I sat, Hammy escaped my pocket and started running away! I chased him and caught him right by a huge tree with branches that reached all the way to the top! A smile spread across my face as I placed Hammy in my pocket.

"Let's go!" I cried out.

I grabbed the tree and started climbing. About a minute later, I was standing on the top of the mountain, proud as a sailor who had just discovered a new island.

"We did it!" I cried at the top of my lungs. Birds flew away. I should have felt offended, but all I felt was pride. I was happy, but I wondered how long we would take to get back down. Just then I noticed a river, a sharp rock, and a log . . .

"Yahooooooooooooo!" I yelled as we went down the river in the log I had hollowed out with the rock. "We should be down in no time. Thanks, Hammy!"

A few minutes later, I saw the lake poke over the trees and a rush of joy came over me when I saw my house, standing out from the rest, welcoming me back.

"Kate is back!" the farmer called from his musty-smelling barn. His shout alerted all the villagers, and they came running from their posts. A crowd came swarming around me, buzzing out questions like bees buzzing around a flower.

"Did you do it?" "Did you climb to the top?" "Where's Hammy?" "Was it scary?" "Can we name the mountain after you?" "What was it like?"

Question after question piled up onto me, and I answered as many as I could.

"Yes, I climbed to the top and it was a bit scary. Hammy is safe! I think we should name the mountain after him!"

"Okay!" Everyone said at once.

Hammy popped his fluffy, grey head out and squeaked wearily. Then my dad, tall, with neat hair like a grizzly and eyes as blue as the sky, much like mine, strode up to me. My frost-colored eyes trembled, as well as my knees, as I gazed into his eyes, steady as a rock gazing back at mine. For a second I thought he would be angry at me for climbing the mountain, but then he scooped me up into a hug.

He hugged me like a cobra grasping its prey, then he planted a warm kiss on my cheek.

"I am very proud of you, Kate. You did a great job," he told me, beaming.

"Thank you," I whispered.

"Do you want a greater challenge?" he asked, a mischievous look in his eye.

I nodded my head, my whole body smiling.

"Then climb that mountain!" he said with a chuckle, pointing to a mountain that I had never noticed, shooting out of the ground on the other side of the village.

Now I could feel my whole body groaning, but I smiled, Hammy squeaking rapidly in my pocket.

"Sure," I replied, facing the mountain, the confidence noticeable in my voice. "I climbed Mt. Hammy, and I will climb you!"

Rainbow

By Ethan Edwards, 9
New York, NY

Rain dripping down fast
from dark and gloomy clouds
the ground a big mirror
suddenly, clouds brighten
and rainbows appear.

Supreme Sunshine (iPhone 11 Pro)
Sabrina Lu, 13
Ashburn, VA

The Earthy World

By Olivia Wang, 10
Atlanta, GA

River water ripples like a smooth glass surface.
Crickets play the drums while birds sing a joyful song.
The sun leaves the sky and leaves no trace,
The moon rises and dances along.
Rain droplets fall to make many things new,
And flowers bloom like fireworks.
Fresh leaves decorated with dew,
Stones sink, not floating like a cork.
The natural scent of sweet lavender—
The smell of nature fills the air.
Waterfalls drop from the sky and meet the river.
Butterflies fly in their home, the sky, an animal fair—
The dreams of nature all come true.
The clouds quietly float in the sky so blue.

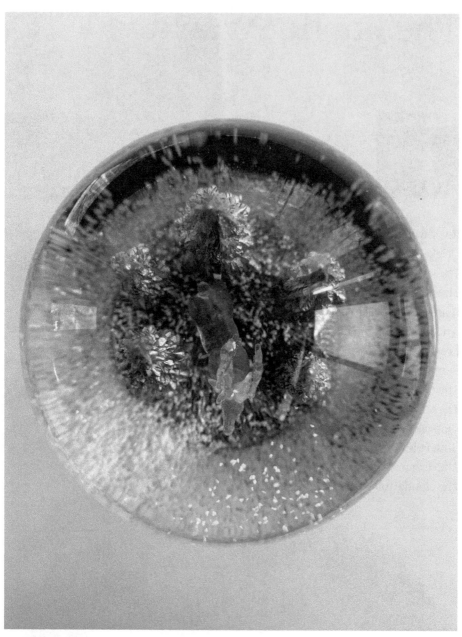

Desolation (iPhone 11 Pro)
Sabrina Lu, 13
Ashburn, VA

Memories

After learning he has only a few days left live, a man looks back on his life

By Renee Wang, 13
Champaign, IL

Theodore Colin looked out from his too-small chair in his roach-ridden room. The majestic cherry tree stood outside, greeting him as always. It was the only color in his life; his retirement home was as grey as his soul.

He recalled, as if it was seared into his brain, what his doctor had told him yesterday: he would have only a few days to live. As he'd dragged his feet back to his room, he could hear his nurse weeping, and when he'd told his friends yesterday, a few tears trickled down their faces. As he'd delivered the news to his sister, his only living relative, he could remember the silence that had followed. It was ironically loud. When he had gotten back to his prison, he sat down at his chessboard, randomly moving pieces about. He pushed it away in disgust.

But even though the news saddened those close to him, he himself did not grieve. That night, his eyes were sore from staring into space. He could feel the chronic illness eating through him like a mold. It had gnawed at him unflinchingly for so many years, consuming the very thing that was keeping him alive. He rubbed his head and looked up. Again, the flowering cherry tree that stood outside his window was there to smile at him. Even though it was painfully pink, the same color as the cancer that was killing him, its long branches swayed like grass, waving to him, inviting him to relive the memories of his glorious younger days. Suddenly, he was hit with a snowball of nostalgia as he was brought back into his memories.

It was a bright shining day as he skipped home from school, spirits high. He could remember the distinct smell of the cherry blossoms that bloomed in the spring, always there to provide him with delicious fruit.

And as the petals of that first cherry tree floated off, turning from a brilliant pink to a muddy orange, he could remember the Christmas Eve of his nightmares. He was stuck at home with a fever choking him, a cup of cod-liver oil by his bedside. Jealousy plagued him, hearing the joyous cries of his friends as they threw snowballs at each other and built snowmen while he wiped snot off his face with his sleeve.

But those hours of suffering had

been only a wisp in his memory as he entered his golden years. So many things had happened in his twenties. It was the bliss of his life—booming business, new inventions. It was like the beautiful cherry tree.

Then one rusty nail had ruined his happy daze: his friend's doom. The Pearl Harbor attacks sealed William Smith's fate. Theodore could recall the day he went to visit him. The hospital was white, too white. As he walked into his room and saw his friend on crutches and a deep scar on his face, there was a feeling of helplessness that ate at him the same way his cancer was doing now.

They conversed on matters of little importance. But it was the shrill, shrill shriek from the neighboring room, followed by uncontrollable sobbing, that popped the bubble shielding Theodore. The feeling that there was a killer in white, blending in with the surroundings, being deceptively unalarming, still haunted him today. He could remember the cloud slowly devouring his friend, just like the illness he now had. He could see his future, the future of their friendship, being swallowed by this shadow. The Angel of Death was looming over him, ready to pounce when he was weakest.

He'd backed out of the room, not bothering to answer or even say goodbye as his friend called after him, his face a mirror of confusion. He could remember the suffocating feeling he felt as he realized that Death would not let his friend live. At the beginning of their encounter, William had promised him that he would be fine. But Theodore realized that the promise was only a mirage, an illusion.

All promises were just illusions.

After he'd recovered from the terrible blow from the double-edged sword of friendship, he married Mae Tate. He was happy, business was exploding, and he was finally about to settle down with a family in Miami. But he smiled with remorse at the naïveté of his early days. How the tables would turn with time.

He remembered how small arguments and tight smiles exchanged at breakfast turned into screaming matches that pounded on his ears and morale. After two years of spat insults and hostile glares, Mae left. At the time, he didn't understand why. He knew, deep in his heart, that they were both good people. But they were bishops of two different colors. Bishops . . .

Chess. Oh, how he loved that game! In the days before his time was stolen by painful headaches, he enjoyed a particular fascination with it. He would watch in wonder as great chess players rose to the occasion, setting new records and breaking the glass ceiling that constrained the game. He reviewed the brilliant games they created from nothing, how their seemingly simple moves crushed their opponents' defenses as if they were made of sand. Who knew something so amazing could rise out of a simple touch of the hand to wooden pieces.

But he also recalled the terror he felt when each of his champions was struck down and replaced with a more cautious player. There were no more resonating queen sacrifices that broke down the defense. There were no more aggressive and bold tactics. It was a new era. Chess had been his comfort, and now, seeing chess transform from a romantic and elegant game into something calculated and robotic shattered his heart. He hadn't felt this broken since seeing his friend's doom.

Thinking back on all this, in his too-small chair and roach-ridden room, he wondered, "Why did it matter?"

He sighed and turned his eyes to the cherry tree. It was beginning to blossom. To him, it seemed like the only thing in the world immune to the tortures of time.

Nothing

By Jake Sun, 9
Winchester, MA

Nothing, a void, a thing you can't just put in an empty vase.
Nothing, not a thing, you can't lock it in a case.
You can't say it is, and once you embrace,
it becomes something, and is just empty space.
Nothing, not tangible, just a void without a face.

Nothing, a place that isn't here.
Nothing, changing our lives, yet not ever there.
A blank screen, outer space, even in the air.
It seems to appear everywhere. It causes great despair.
Nothing is the place you get to at nowhere.
Maybe, just maybe, it can be we're unaware,
unaware of the greatness that ensnares
the darkness of the fact that nothing's there.

It helps us when we need to think, or if we're surrounded in a county fair.
Appearing at its best, it can help us pass a test, or live through a war.
Nothing, at its purest, is extremely rare.
When we're working, we are very aware
of every single sound that is emitted through the air.

Underneath (iPhone 6)
Anna Weinberg, 11
Washington, DC

Highlights from Stonesoup.com

From the Stone Soup Blog

Book Review:
How to Sharpen Pencils
by David Rees

By Brais Macknik-Conde, 11
Brooklyn NY

How to Sharpen Pencils: A Practical & Theoretical Treatise on the Artisanal Craft of Pencil Sharpening for Writers, Artists, Contractors, Flange Turners, Anglesmiths, & Civil Servants by David Rees, is a gold mine for anyone wishing to sharpen a pencil. David Rees is a celebrated cartoonist, television host, writer, and artist. From listing the essential supplies for pencil sharpening (at a reasonable $1,000!) to describing the anatomy of a pencil, to explaining how to preserve a freshly sharpened tip, this manual has it all. This truly is the ultimate guide to pencil sharpening.

Rees's guide walks the reader through different sharpening styles and how they may apply to different styles of people and professions. One of my favorite sections describes how to sharpen a pencil with a pocketknife. For example, he recommends producing a steep-angled pencil tip for people with heavy hands, as this will make it harder to break the tip off. He also advises exposing a lot of the graphite in pencils for artists, as this will make for a light sketch that can be easily erased.

Rees's love of manual pencil sharpening is only surpassed by his hatred of electric pencil sharpening and mechanical pencils. Here is one hint: Rees's feelings about electric pencil sharpeners involve the use of mallets.

Without giving away all of this guide's secrets, I must mention Rees's most prized pencil-sharpening possession: an El Casco M430-CN. Created by a company that once made firearms, this double-burr hand-cranked machine, Rees declares, is the best pencil sharpener on Earth.

I enjoyed reading Rees's tongue-in-check manual not just for its jokes and wisecracks, but also for its factual information, and even its lifestyle recommendations. By reading this book, I have learned the proper hand-stretching exercises to do before long pencil-sharpening sessions, that a correctly sharpened pencil is an object of beauty, and that mechanical pencils make for good firewood. This book is where I will always look to for pencil-sharpening guidance and inspiration, and it is where you should too.

About the Stone Soup Blog

On the Stone Soup Blog, we publish original work—writing, art, book reviews, multimedia projects, and more—by young people. You can read more posts by young bloggers, and find out more about submitting a blog post, here: https://stonesoup.com/stone-soup-blog/.

Honor Roll

Welcome to the Stone Soup Honor Roll. Every month, we receive submissions from hundreds of kids from around the world. Unfortunately, we don't have space to publish all the great work we receive. We want to commend some of these talented writers and artists and encourage them to keep creating.

STORIES

Filzah Affan, 6
Sol Chung, 9
Aashi Gupta, 10
Carolina Henderson, 10
Sofia Huntley, 6
Olivia Hush, 12
Sophia Li, 10
Samuel Liang, 6
Alma Mendez, 12
Mia Shazeer, 8
Andrea Shi, 13
David Yu, 11

ART

Shiloh David, 4
Angelica C. Gary, 10
Eva Humphris, 12
Sela Milgrom-Dorfman, 11
Ainsley Rhoton, 13

POETRY

Tarun Chava, 13
Priscilla Chow, 7
Hava Goldfinger, 8
Penn Kerhoulas, 7
Jaya Khurana, 10
Iris Kindseth, 10
Georgia Marshall, 12
Madeline Smith, 8
Kalyani Spieckerman, 12

PERSONAL NARRATIVE

Edward Antwi, 12
Matthew Fic, 12
Eleanor Moy, 11
Tyler Oberdorf, 12
Deniz Ozsirkinti, 11
Ramona Weinstein, 11

Visit the *Stone Soup* Store at Stonesoupstore.com

At our store, you will find . . .

- Current and back issues of *Stone Soup* Magazine

- Our growing collection of books by young authors, as well as themed anthologies and the *Stone Soup Annual*

- High-quality prints from our collection of children's art

- Journals and sketchbooks

. . . and more!

Finally, don't forget to visit Stonesoup.com to browse our bonus materials. There you will find:

- More information about our writing workshops and book club

- Monthly flash contests and weekly creativity prompts

- Blog posts from our young bloggers on everything from sports to sewing

- Video interviews with *Stone Soup* authors

. . . and more content by young creators!

CPSIA information can be obtained
at www.ICGtesting.com
Printed in the USA
BVHW050302070921
616116BV00001B/3